Chapter 1

Abigail

It's the first day of school holidays. Abigail has just awoken and can tell it's going to be another warm day. The sun is shining through the curtains. She jumps up, quickly getting dressed. She bounds downstairs for her breakfast, taking the steps two at a time. She wants to enjoy every minute of the seven-week school holidays.

'Morning, Abigail,' says her mum. 'You are up bright and early this morning.'

THE HOLIDAY

OF ADVENTURE AND

MAGIC

Aileen Nisbet

Table of Content

Chapter 1 Abigail 4

Chapter 2 Hannah 26

Chapter 3 Becky..............................37

Chapter 4 Jodie...............................54

Chapter 5 Abigail 68

Chapter 6 Hannah 82

Chapter 7 Becky..............................95

Chapter 8 Jodie...............................113

Chapter 9 Abigail 147

Chapter 10 Mrs Harper..................151

Chapter 11 Robyn.........................165

'Yes, I am,' says Abigail excitedly. 'I am meeting my friends down at the promenade at 10 o'clock this morning. We are going exploring.'

Abigail's brother Rory is stuffing his face with cereal like there is no tomorrow. He looks up from his bowl, milk dribbling down his chin. He wipes it with his sleeve. 'Where are you four going exploring?' he asks.

'Down on the beach amongst the rocks,' Abigail replies. 'Can't wait. There is always something happening when we go.'

'More like you four always get into trouble when you get together,' Rory replies. He drops his spoon in his bowl, slides his chair away from the table and says, 'Well, I'm finished. See you later, Abigail. Try not to get into too much trouble.'

Abigail finishes her breakfast and rushes out of the house. She strolls down the promenade, so glad she put her shorts on. It's almost 10 o'clock and already getting warm. It's a glorious morning. Families are heading for the beach with towels under their arms, bats and balls to play with on the beach, and the occasional inflatable.

Abigail has a spring in her step. Today is just perfect and the sun is shining. She is going to meet her three best friends: Jodie, Becky and Hannah.

They are all ten years old except for Becky, who will be ten next month.

Abigail arrives at the pier and can see Hannah on her way towards her. They both give an excited wave. Hannah arrives and they both sit on the wall, legs dangling over the edge, looking out to sea.

'Do you think this year will be as exciting as last year?' Hannah asks.

'Let's hope so,' Abigail replies.

They then hear the giggles of Jodie and Becky. They both turn round and see their friends making their way across the road towards the pier.

Abigail and Hannah swing round from the wall and get off.

Abigail shouts for a group hug for the four best friends. They all stand in a huddle, arms round each other. They count to five, and then they all high five each other.

'Let's get on the beach!' Jodie shouts. 'What are we waiting for?'

They all climb onto the wall one by one, then jump down onto the sand. They each look at one another and laugh.

'It's going to be a great summer,' Abigail says.

They start to run towards the sea. They take their socks and trainers off and go for a paddle. They stroll along the water's edge, just enough to get their feet and ankles wet. They come to the rocky part of the beach.

Becky shouts, 'Let's see who can find a shell you can hear the sea in first!'

They all start to wander, looking for the best shell.

Jodie shouts, 'I've found half of one!'

Becky replies, 'That doesn't count. You can't hear the sea from that.'

They all fall about laughing. They clamber about the rocks all morning, heading further down the coast.

Hannah ends up lagging behind. She stumbles and goes over on her ankle.

She shouts, 'I've hurt my ankle!'

They all come running to her aid.

'Are you okay?' Abigail asks.

'Yes,' Hannah laughs. 'Trust me.' Just as Hannah is getting back to her feet, she notices a cluster of strange, large rocks that she's never seen before. It's mostly the shape of them that catches her eye. 'Look,' she says, pointing. 'What's that over there? I've never noticed these rocks before.'

They all wander over to get a closer look. There are a lot of pyramid-shaped rocks. They wander round, following what appears to be a pathway. The path winds round and round, passing pyramid-shaped rocks of all sizes. The path comes to an abrupt end. There is one large pyramid right in front of them, with a door-like opening covered with pieces of wood.

Hannah says, 'What is this? Why does it have a door? The wood on the door looks like it could have been boarded up for a few years.'

They all stand and stare, curious as to what it is.

Abigail says, 'I don't think we have ever walked this far round the coast before. Let's see if we can get the wood off and see what's inside.'

They each start to tug at the wood. The first couple of pieces come off relatively easily. There are still four large pieces nailed together. Jodie pulls very hard at the largest piece and ends up with a splinter in her finger.

'Watch what you are doing!' Abigail shouts.

Becky had been standing watching them, she says, 'We need to go find something to help prise the wood off.'

Becky and Hannah decide they will go look while Abigail and Jodie stay. They continue to tug and pull at the wood. Eventually, they manage to remove another two pieces, leaving just two remaining. They sit down for a rest and wait for Becky and Hannah to return. They eventually appear with a large piece of metal that looks like it could have belonged to a car.

Becky shouts, 'Look, girls, at what we have herc! Surely this will help!'

Using the piece of metal between them, they manage to prise the remaining two pieces off. They all let out a cheer.

Abigail pops her head in first but says, 'It's too dark. I can't see anything.'

The other three have a look too, but it's no good. It's way too dark.

'We need a torch,' says Abigail. 'I will run home and get one. My dad keeps one under the stairs in case we have power cuts.'

Jodie says, 'I will come with you. I'm sure there must be one somewhere in my house too.'

They run excitedly back along the coast till they come to the wall that they can climb over to get back onto the promenade. They run along the pavement, going to Jodie's house first. Jodie has a rummage in a cupboard where she thinks she might find a torch, with no luck.

'I will go and ask my mum,' she says to Abigail. 'She's sitting out in the back garden.'

Abigail stops her. 'No, she might stop us from going back. Let's go to my house. I know there is definitely one in the cupboard under the stairs.'

They reach Abigail's house. H
is in the front garden attending
weeds.

'Hi girls!' she shouts. 'You're back early. Where's the other two?'

Abigail thinks quickly. 'We are just back for bats and balls to play with on the beach. Hannah and Becky are waiting there for us.'

'Okay' her mum shouts. 'I think you will find them in the cupboard under the stairs.' She carries on with her weeding.

Abigail runs in, grabs Rory's old sports bag, and puts four bats and balls in the bag. She finds the torch.

'Is it working?' Jodie asks.

Abigail tries it. 'Yes, it is,' she says, shining it right in Jodie's face. 'Let's get out of here.' They go back out to the garden, making sure the bats are sticking out of the bag.

'Bye mum!' Abigail says. 'I will be back for dinner.'

They hurry back down to the beach, climb the wall, and jump back down onto the sand. The beach seems really busy at this end. They start to walk along the beach again, heading to where they left the others.

Jodie says, 'I can't remember walking along as far as this. You sure we haven't missed the rocks?'

Abigail says, 'No. We did walk a lot further round the coast than we normally do.'

The beach is getting quieter thc further round they walk. This end is not as popular. They keep walking till they are the only two on the beach for miles. Eventually they see the strangely-shaped rocks again and head over.

Hannah and Becky have wandered back round the pathway to watch for them. Hannah spots them first and shouts, 'Over here! Did you get a torch?'

Abigail says, 'Yes! Let's go and see what's in there.'

They follow the path in a single file line back round to the large pyramid at the end. Abigail bends down and flashes the torch inside. She shouts, 'There are things in here! Someone else has been here. I can see a table and lots of chairs. There is a bag sitting on the table, or it could be a case. I'm not sure. There are a lot of lanterns dotted about on the ground.'

Becky shouts, 'Let's all go in! You go first, Abigail, with the torch.'

Hannah says, 'If someone has been living here, they haven't got very much.'

Jodie points. 'What are those things in the corner? They are like large cupboards with large sliding doors.'

Abigail wanders over with the torch. 'I haven't a clue. They look a bit like tan stands but without the florescent tubes.'

Hannah says, 'Shine the torch over here at the table. Let's see what this bag is.'

It turns out to be an old case. Hannah tries to open it, but it's locked. There is a padlock preventing it from opening. It is the kind where the numbers must be lined up correctly to unlock.

Abigail points out, 'Even if we get the numbers correct, will it open it's so old.'

Becky sighs. 'It's a pity we don't have batteries to light these lanterns. Then we would be able to see better what we are doing.'

Abigail notices what she thinks is a picture on the wall. 'Look, girls, what's this?' She goes over and they all follow her. They see that it is a calendar. All the pictures on it are of outer space. 'Strange pictures to have on a calendar,' she says.

Jodie says, 'Look at the year on it: 1970. That's over fifty years ago. Why would someone have a calendar in here and why is it so old?'

Hannah says, 'Let's look at this case again.' They all move towards it, Abigail leading with the torch.

Abigail says, 'We are all so stupid. We don't need to know the number combination or have a key. Why don't we just burst the case open with a knife or cut the material with scissors? It doesn't look particularly sturdy. It's really old.'

'One problem,' Jodie says. 'We don't have either scissors or a knife.'

Hannah says, 'Why don't Becky and I run home and get some scissors? We could also check for batteries to light these lanterns.' They run off to fetch these items.

Abigail and Jodie wander around, trying to make sense of everything.

Abigail says, 'All may become clearer when we get the case open.'

They each take a seat. Abigail shines the torch round the place. Abigail asks what the time is. Jodie replies that its 4 o'clock

'Oh, we are going to run out of time!' claims Abigail. 'I have to be home by 6 o'clock for my dinner.'

It's five o'clock before Hannah and Becky appear back. They have managed to get three torches, four pairs of scissors and a selection of batteries. They switch all the torches on and lay them on the floor. They each take a pair of scissors and dig into the material on the case. It's tougher than it looks. They manage to burst their way through some of the material, but still can't quite get into it.

Jodie has the biggest pair of scissors and says, 'Let me have a go at it.'

She manages to dig in and remove a part of the case material. They all take turns, as it's hurting their hands. They eventually get in and pull back the rest of the material. There's a photo of a young man. It must be from a long time ago because his clothes are old-fashioned, his hair is long, and he has a beard. There are two books inside, one on outer space and one on teleporters.

'What is a teleporter?' asks Jodie.

'Is that not when you can transport an object from one place to another?' says Abigail. 'Rory did a lesson at school on this. He told me all about it.'

Hannah then notices an envelope. 'What's this?' she asks. She grabs it and pulls it out. 'It's a bit dusty. Looks like it's been in there for a while.'

Abigail asks the time again. Jodie replies that it's almost 6 o'clock..

'I will have to go home for my dinner,' Abigail says.

They all agree it's time to go.

Hannah says, 'I will take the envelope home and read. It's probably just the man's diary of his time in here.'

They all scramble to their feet, shining the torches. Once outside, they sit the planks of wood back against the door to try to hide it. They run back along the coast to where they can climb over the wall and back onto the promenade. They agree to meet again tomorrow at ten o'clock at their usual spot. Hannah tells them she will read the letter in the envelope that night and fill them in tomorrow. They each go their separate ways.

Chapter 2

Hannah

Hannah strolls along the promenade with the letter firmly in her hands, checking every so often that it's still there. She's curious and excited, wondering what it says. She arrives home.

'Hi, Hannah!' her mum shouts from the kitchen. 'Your dinner will be ready in fifteen minutes, so you have time to get washed.'

'Okay,' Hannah replies.

She runs upstairs and looks around her room, wondering where to put the letter to keep it safe until she has time to read it. She decides to put it in a shoe box in the bottom of her wardrobe. She wraps it in the tissue paper from the box, puts it under the shoes in the box, puts the lid back on, and places a few bags on top of the box. She wonders why she is going to all this bother when no one knows it's there.

She gets washed and goes downstairs for dinner. It's only Hannah and her mum, as her dad is still at work. He's a bus driver and does different shifts. Hannah can't wait to finish her dinner so she can go upstairs and read the letter.

'No pudding for me tonight, Mum. I'm full up,' Hannah says as she leaves the table. She runs upstairs to get the shoe box and unwraps the letter from the tissue paper. She takes it out and begins to read.

Hello,

If you are reading this letter, then you have found my secret cave and I am most probably not

around. This is more than likely due to my invention, a teleporter. 1 invented this device to

prove to everyone that you can teleport human beings and not just objects. I haven't quite got it perfect yet—a few bits of the machine still need worked on. I will say, though, that it does work and if you do decide to use it, you must always take someone else with you.

Cheers

Robyn

Hannah sits down and stares at the letter, not quite sure what to make of it. An invention—in that case, where is it and how does it work?

Hannah's heart is racing. She can't wait to tell the others. She looks at the alarm clock in her room. It's only ten minutes past eight o'clock. How can she make the night go faster? She so wants tomorrow morning to come as soon as possible. She doesn't want to risk phoning or texting in case the message is seen by someone's parents, who may put a stop to their adventure. She will just have to wait till tomorrow to tell all.

She tells her mum she is going to bed early because she is tired from running around on the beach and wants to read. She gets ready for bed and picks up her book, hoping it will make her tired. She can't concentrate on it, though, because she keeps thinking about the letter. She puts her book down and reaches under her bed for the box where the letter is, and reads it again and again till she's so tired. She ends up putting the letter under her pillow and eventually falls asleep.

She awakens early the next morning and feels under her pillow for the letter. It's there. It's real, not a dream. She gets up, gets ready and goes downstairs. For breakfast she has a bowl of cereal and some fresh orange juice.

'What are your plans for today, Hannah?' her mum asks.

'I'm meeting the others at ten o'clock and we are going down to the beach again.'

'That's nice,' replies her mum. 'It's a lovely day for it.'

Hannah heads for the beach to meet the others. She arrives first, so she has a seat on the wall. The sun is shining today. A man walks past with a poodle and says good morning. She looks round and can see the others running towards her.

'Well?' Abigail shouts from a distance. 'Did you read it?'

'Yes!' Hannah shouts back.

They all arrive and sit on the wall beside Hannah. 'What did it say?' they ask.

Hannah reads the letter to them. When she is finished, no one says a word. They just sit and look at one another.

Jodie eventually breaks the silence. 'Come on, let's go back to the cave and investigate. Oh, and I have three nightlights that work with batteries.'

'Brilliant!' Abigail shouts. 'Let's go!'

They all run along the beach. Abigail has a picnic with her for everyone to enjoy, which her mum made for them since yesterday she had complained that they had no lunch. They eventually reach the cave and move the pieces of wood away from the doorway. They all switch their torches on, and Jodie switches all the nightlights on too.

Becky is the first to speak. 'What's the invention? How does it work and where is it?' She gets up and walks round the room with her torch. She stops when she gets to the two objects that look like tan stands, though that's definitely not what they are.

Hannah shouts, 'Be careful, Becky! We don't know how this works yet.'

Becky ignores her and steps inside one of the objects. Curiosity has gotten the better of her. She shuts the door, laughing, and says, 'Teleport me to Disneyland, please.' She presses the green button on the top of the door. There is also a red lever at the bottom of the door, but she doesn't touch that.

All of a sudden, there is a grumbling noise. The unit shakes about and everyone can hear the screams from Becky.

Jodie shouts, 'Don't fool around, Becky! It's not funny! You don't know what you are dealing with!' They all run towards the unit where Becky is. Jodie pulls at the door, but it won't open. The grumbling noise is getting louder.

'Becky!' she shouts. 'Are you still in there?'

They all start to panic when there is no answer.

'What's happened? She must still be in there!' Abigail screams.

Eventually the grumbling noise stops. Abigail pulls at the door. It opens this time, but Becky is not there.

Chapter 3

Becky

Becky finds herself sitting on a bench with candy floss in her hand. She has no idea where she is or how she got there. Her heart is racing. She starts to panic and is on the verge of crying.

A young boy is standing in front of her. He is probably about five years of age. 'What's wrong with you?' he asks. 'Why are you not happy? You are at Disneyland. Everyone is happy when they are here.'

She gives him a dirty look and he runs off.

'Disneyland,' she says out loud. 'How did I get here?' Then she remembers the cave and the teleporter. 'I pressed the green button. Oh no, what am I going to do? How am I going to get back home?' She gets up from the seat, holding onto the candy floss. She starts to walk round. The place is so busy, with lots of laughter and screaming coming from the rides. She thinks, 'Is it Disneyland Paris or Florida? I don't even know.' She tries to listen to people's conversations, especially the people who work there, and comes to the conclusion that she's in the Florida

Disneyland. 'Oh no, what am I going to do? I have no money, no mobile phone, and I'm stranded.' She decides to eat the candy floss. It does look good, after all.

She wanders around, and then suddenly a large Mickey Mouse appears in front of her. 'You on your own, young girl? Are you lost?' He takes her hand. 'Let me show you round while we look for your parents. What is your name?'

'Becky.' She tries to explain she is not with her parents, but the noise around them and his costume prevent him from hearing her properly.

Mickey Mouse tries to cheer her up. 'Would you like to try and win a prize by hooping a duck?' he asks.

'Yes, okay,' Becky replies. Then she says, 'Oh, but I don't have any money.'

'Dont worry let me pay,' Mickey replies. Becky tries several times to win a prize, with no luck.

Mickey then says, 'Have you had your breakfast?'

'Why, yes, ages ago,' Becky replies whilst looking at her watch. 'Its three o'clock in the afternoon.'

'No, little lady, it's actually only ten o'clock in the morning,' Mickey says.

Becky tells him she is from the UK, and he says that there is a five-hour time difference between the UK and Florida. Mickey asks, 'Where are you from in the UK?'

'Ayr in Scotland,' Becky replies.

'Oh, look!' Mickey shouts. 'The bumper cars! Would you like to go on? I love the bumpers.'

'Yes, okay,' Becky says.

They both squeeze into one car. There is not much room with Mickey's bulky outfit.

Becky thinks to herself, 'This is crazy. How did I get to Florida?' Her heart starts to race again, her hands are clammy, and she wonders how she will get home. 'Will I see my mum and dad ever again?' she thinks. 'Oh, and my big sister Cheryl and my three best friends, Abigail, Hannah and Jodie. Do they even know what's happened to me? Are they trying to get me home? Stupid teleporter! I wish I had never seen the thing.'

Just then, she gets a jolt as the bumper cars start to move. Mickey is really good at driving. He manages to miss two head-on collisions. Another car is heading their way. He swerves and avoids that one too, obviously having had plenty of practice. Becky shrieks with laughter. Mickey is so much fun to be with that, for a moment, she forgets she is lost and enjoys herself. Once out of the car, she stands with her hands in her pockets, fiddling with the broken candy floss stick in her pocket.

Mickey turns to her and says, 'This way, Becky.' He heads over to where a small boy is standing crying. He looks a little younger than Becky. Mickey bends down. 'Hello, little boy. Are you lost? What's your name?'

Through uncontrollable sobs, he manages to say, 'Adam.'

'Who are you with?' Mickey asks.

'My dad,' the little boy answers.

Mickey gets what information he can from Adam and radios in to the lost children's area, just like he did for Becky.

'Right now, no more crying,' Mickey says. 'We will find your dad. Take my other hand. This is Becky. She is also lost. We will wander round, and if anyone is looking for either of you, the office will radio me. We can then arrange a meeting place.' They walk past the water logs and Mickey asks, 'Who doesn't mind getting wet?'

Becky and Adam both shout, 'I don't!'

'Right, let's have a go, then.'

They all get on. Becky is in the front, Adam is in the middle, and Mickey is in the back. Becky suddenly realises she is going to get the worst of the splashes, but she doesn't mind. It will be fun. Adam and Becky have a great laugh. They are both soaked through, and there's water dripping from Becky's hair. Mickey's huge costume kept him dry. They get off and climb back down the stairs. Becky puts her hand in her pocket to see if she has a hanky to dry her face, but all she has is the broken candy floss stick. She pulls it out, ready to try and find a bin for it, when she notices there is a message on it. While Mickey is on his radio, she reads it. It says, 'To get home, go back to where you arrived.'

'What on earth does that mean?' Becky asks herself. 'Back to where I arrived'

Tears fill her eyes, as the message is a sharp reminder of the mess she's in.

Just then, Adam pulls at her arm and Mickey's too. 'Over there!' he shouts. 'It is my dad!' Mickey goes over to the man. He asks the man, 'Are you looking for anyone?'

'Yes,' the man says loudly. He looks at Adam. 'Where have you been?'

Mickey says, 'We will have to go to the lost children's office and fill in some forms.'

They head back round the way they came, past the bumper cars and the hoop-a-duck game. When they pass the bench Becky arrived on, she notices a scrunched-up piece of paper on the bench. She grabs it as she walks past, wondering if the message on the candy floss stick meant for her to go back to the bench where she arrived. She slips the paper into her pocket.

They arrive at the lost children's office. Mickey says, 'You have a seat there, Becky, while I fill in the forms with Adam and his dad. I won't be long.'

Becky takes a seat. When the others are engrossed in the forms, she takes the scrunched-up piece of paper from her pocket.

The message reads: For a return journey, you must go back to where you arrived.

'That's the bench,' Becky thinks.

The message continues: You will become invisible as soon as you reach the spot where you arrived, and no one will be able to hear you. You must say the following words: please teleport me back to the hideaway cave. Once you say these words, you will end up back in the teleporter. I hope you remembered that you always need two people for a return journey. You can begin your teleportation on your own, as you only need to say where you want to go and press the green button. For a return journey, however, you need to repeat the words when you are back inside the teleporter while at the same time turning the red lever at the bottom of the door and pressing the green button at the top of the door. Unless you are tall like me, it will be impossible to do on your own.

'Oh no,' Becky thinks, 'I'm on my own. Will I be able to press the button at the top and turn the lever at the bottom on my own? I have to try.'

Becky looks up. Mickey is still helping Adam and his dad with the paperwork. She thinks fast, wondering if she could escape back to the bench where she arrived without Mickey noticing she's gone. She gets up from her seat as quietly as possible and moves to the door. She has folded the instructions and is holding on to them very tightly.

They are her ticket home. She manages to escape. Mickey doesn't notice her slipping out the door. She feels bad for leaving without thanking Mickey for taking care of her. He was so kind to her.

She quickly runs back round to the bench. There's a woman sitting on it. 'Oh no,' Becky thinks, 'get off of it.' She then remembers that as soon as she reaches the point where the teleporter dropped her off, she will be invisible and no one will hear her. She walks towards the bench.

The woman smiles at her and says, 'Hello. Would you like a seat?'

'Arggh,' Becky thinks, 'I'm not invisible at all.' She sits down, turns to the woman, and says, 'Hi, my name is Becky.' The woman is looking in the opposite direction and doesn't answer her. She tries again. 'Hi, my name is Becky.' The woman still looks the other way and doesn't answer. 'Am I really invisible?' Becky laughs. 'If I wasn't so worried about getting home, I could have a lot of fun with this.' She tests it one more time. She shouts to a man walking past with his daughter. 'Hi, don't I know you?' They both walk straight past her. They smile at the woman next to her. 'I must really be invisible. I wonder if I'll still be invisible if I get off the bench.' She jumps off, looks at the woman next to her, and says, 'Hi.'

The woman smiles and replies, 'Hi. Are you lost? Why are you on your own?'

'Okay,' Becky thinks, 'I must stay on the bench to remain invisible.' She sits back down on the bench and can see the woman looking in both directions for her, wondering where she went.

Becky gets the piece of paper out and says, 'Please teleport me back to the hideaway cave on the beach.' The next minute, she finds herself back inside the teleporter. 'Right now I must repeat the words, I think, and at the same time turn the red lever and press the green button.' She repeats the words and starts to turn the lever at the bottom of the door, but can't reach the button at the same time. She tries lying on the floor where she can reach the lever at the bottom and stretches her leg up in the air to try and reach the button, but her legs are too short. She slumps down onto the floor and starts to cry. 'This is hopeless. How am I going to get home on my own?' She sobs herself to sleep on the floor.

Chapter 4

Jodie

Meanwhile, back at the cave, Abigail, Jodie and Hannah are all huddled together outside the teleporter, wondering what on earth to do.

'It's now five o'clock,' Abigail says. 'Becky has been gone for hours. We are all due to go home for our dinner at six, and Becky isn't here. What will we tell her mum?'

Hannah says, 'We have to work out a way to get her back. Where is that old case? Check that there's nothing else in it, like instructions.'

They flick through the two books about space and teleportation, to see if they can find any more information, but there is nothing.

Hannah reads the letter from the case again. 'It mentions that there must always be at least two people to use the teleporter,' she says. 'I wonder why it worked fine with just Becky in it on her own. It certainly sent her off to Disneyland.'

Jodie says, 'That's it! One of us will need to go in the teleporter too and say exactly what Becky said, and hopefully end up at the same destination.'

Abigail asks, 'What did she say, again? Can anyone remember?'

'She said "Please transport me to Disneyland" and the teleporter rumbled and shook about and then there was no Becky," Hannah says.

'Who wants to go, then?' Abigail asks. No one says a word. No one wants to go, as they are all afraid they too will end up stranded somewhere.

Eventually, Jodie says, 'I will go. Just remember, if I don't come back soon, something has gone wrong.'

'Oh,' Abigail says, 'we have forty-five minutes till dinner time. Hopefully this will work and we can all be home in time.'

'Wait a minute,' Hannah says. 'Why don't we phone Becky on her mobile?' They all laugh. 'Why did we not think of this sooner?' Abigail says. She gets her mobile out and phones Becky. Much to their disappointment, though, they can hear Becky's phone ringing. She didn't take it with her.

'Right,' Jodie says. 'There's nothing else for it, I will have to try and find Becky. I will take my mobile with me so I can call you with any information.' Jodie gets in the teleporter and nervously shuts the door.

'Are you okay, Jodie?' Hannah asks.

'Yes,' Jodie replies, 'I think so.'

Hannah and Abigail can hear Jodie say the words 'please take me to Disneyland' and then she presses the green button. The teleporter starts to rumble and shake about. Hannah and Abigail jump back from it.

'Oh, it's working again!' Hannah says. 'I hope Jodie is going to be okay.'

Eventually the noise stops. Hannah and Abigail cautiously move towards the teleporter. After it has stopped shaking, Abigail opens the door and sees that Jodie is gone too. Abigail and Hannah just stand staring at the empty teleporter, both at a loss for words.

Jodie finds herself sitting on a bench with a teddy in her hand. 'Where on earth did that come from?' she asks herself. She looks around. She can't believe her eyes. She is really in Disneyland! 'Becky is here somewhere,' she thinks. 'The place is so big and noisy. Where on earth do I start looking?' She gets up from the bench and starts to wander round, still holding the teddy. She passes by a rollercoaster and stands for a minute to watch. She loves roller coasters.

A couple of girls push her. 'Are you in the queue?' they ask.

'No,' she says. 'I'm just watching.'

'Well get out the way!' one of them shouts.

'Charming girls,' Jodie thinks. 'Glad they are not my friends.' She walks off and feels in her pocket for her mobile. 'Best let Hannah and Abigail know I have arrived safely.' She looks at her phone. It is displaying a message saying no service. 'I don't believe it! My phone has no signal here.'

The next minute, a large Minnie Mouse approaches her. 'Are you on your own?' she asks.

'Eh, I've kind of lost my friend,' Jodie says.

'We don't like young ones wandering about here on their own. Take my hand. I will help you look for your friend.

What's your name?' Minnie asks as they squeeze by the crowds.

'It's Jodie.'

'And what's your friend's name?'

'Becky.'

'Okay, I will radio the lost children's office with your details. If they have any information, they will contact me.'

'It's nice of Minnie Mouse to help me, but I really need to try and get away from her,' Jodie thinks. 'How can I explain how Becky and I got here and that our parents are not with us? This nightmare just gets worse.'

They come across the maze of mirrors. Minnie says, 'Would you like a go?'

Jodie thinks, 'What a great place to lose Minnie.' She nods.

They stand in a queue and eventually enter the maze. 'You go first,' Jodie says, 'so I can follow you.' Jodie follows Minnie as they laugh their way through the maze.

'I've done this so many times, Jodie,' Minnie says, 'that I should know it by heart, but time and time again I still get it wrong.'

They both laugh. Jodie decides that the next opportunity she has, she is going to go in a different direction than Minnie. As she does, Minnie doesn't realise and carries on, singing as she goes. Jodie tries to remember the path taken to get back. After all, they haven't gone that far in.

Minnie then realises she's lost Jodie.

'Jodie!' she shouts. 'Where are you?'

Jodie shouts, 'I'm not that far behind you! I took a wrong turn. I will be right there.'

'Oh!' Minnie shouts. 'I will stand still and keep talking so you know what direction to take.'

'Okay!' Jodie shouts back, even though she is heading in the opposite direction. She drops the teddy she arrived with in her panic to get out. She bends down to pick it up and, as she does, sees a note drop out from its back. She picks up the note and the teddy. She manages to get out of the maze and quickly runs for a bit to make sure she's totally out of Minnie's sight.

She finds a bench and has a seat to read the note. It says, 'For a return journey, you must go back to where you arrived.' Jodie thinks, 'Where I arrived? That must be the bench. Oh, I don't know if I can find it again. I will have to retrace my steps.' She walks round and round looking for the exact bench. She remembers that it was near a stall where you had to hoop a duck to win a prize. She eventually finds it, plunks herself down and begins to read the note again. The note explains to her that when she is back where she arrived and repeats the words in the letter, she will become invisible and no one will be able to hear her.

Meanwhile, Becky awakens. Her eyes feel all puffy and sore from crying. She realises right away where she is. 'Oh no, I so hoped this had all been a bad dream, but no, I'm still stuck here. Well, no point in sitting in here. I might as well get back out, as this thing is not going to work while I'm on my own.' She goes for a walk to stretch her legs, and then decides to wander back, afraid that she might bump into Micky. After all, she ran away from him. She sits back on the bench. There's a girl sitting on the bench beside her. 'I wish she would go away,' Becky thinks. 'I don't want to talk to anyone.' The girl drops her teddy. Becky watches her pick it up. 'I can't believe my eyes! It's Jodie! No, it can't be, can it?' Out loud, she says, 'Jodie?'

Jodie screams, 'Becky! At last, I've found you! What happened?'

Becky explains that the teleporter needs two people for the return journey, unless you are tall enough to press the green button at the top of the door and turn the red lever at the bottom of the door at the same time. 'Right, let's get out of here,' Becky says. 'I know what to do. We repeat what's on this note and we will end up back in the teleporter.'

They say the words, and the next thing they know, they are both in the teleporter. 'Right,' Becky says. 'I will say the message and press the green button, if you turn the red lever at the bottom. It has to all be done at the same time for it to work.'

Next thing they know, they are back in the hideaway cave on the beach.

Hannah and Abigail jump when they hear rumbling from the teleporter. When it stops, out pop Becky and Jodie.

Chapter 5

Abigail

Abigail gets home for dinner late that night. By the time Jodie and Becky got back, they were already over an hour late and didn't even have time to discuss what happened. They agreed to meet tomorrow to discuss it. They don't want to talk on their mobiles in case they are overheard, and they don't want to text either in case their parents see. It's their secret and they are not risking the adventures and fun they could have all summer with the teleporter.

They meet up the next morning at ten o'clock as planned. Abigail is there first and can't wait to hear the news. They all run along the beach to the cave and switch on the battery lanterns and torches. Abigail speaks first. 'Right, Becky, Jodie, what happened? Did you really go to Disneyland? Why couldn't you get back, Becky? Why did you not phone us, Jodie, when you got there?' There are so many questions to be answered.

Jodie and Becky tell the story of what happened— how Jodie's mobile didn't work and how you must always go in pairs because you need at least two people to operate the teleporter on the return journey. Abigail and Hannah are so excited and can't believe their stories.

'I can't wait to try it out,' Abigail says. 'Do you think the four of us could go together? Where could we go?'

'That's a great idea,' Jodie says. 'Let's all go together from now on. We could pick a different destination each day and go together on some amazing adventures.'

Abigail asks, 'Can I pick first?'

'Okay!' they all shout, knowing they are all going to get a turn.

Abigail sits and thinks of where she would like to go. 'I'd like us all to go to Blair Drummond Safari Park in

Stirling. I had a great time there last summer with my parents and brother.

'Okay, let's go!' Jodie screams.

They all climb into the teleporter.

Abigail says, 'I will tell the teleporter where we would like to go. Becky, you press the green button and hopefully we will be off.'

They do just that. They start to hear rumbling noises and they are off.

Next thing they know, they are in the middle of the zoo. They arrive seated at a dolphin show. Abigail has a cap on her knee with a picture of a dolphin on it. 'What's this?' she says.

Becky shouts, 'Oh, there will be a note in it! Be careful, Abigail, as that note will be the instructions for our return journey. They could be different this time, as we are at the zoo and not Disneyland.'

Abigail turns it over and, sure enough, there's a note inside.

'Keep it safe,' Hannah says. 'Wait till we are outside to read it. Let's watch the dolphin show.'

After the show, they find a picnic table to sit and listen carefully as Abigail reads the note.

The note reads: For your return journey, you must go back to where you arrived and repeat the following words: please teleport me back to the hideaway cave.

'Okay, we need to keep the note and the cap safe,' Abigail says.

Jodie asks, 'What time is it? How long did our journey take?'

"It's eleven o'clock,' Abigail replies. 'We must have only been at the dolphin show for about twenty minutes. That means the journey must have only taken fifteen minutes, not long at all.'

They sit at the picnic table, watching everyone go by.

'Where will we go first?' Abigail shouts.

'Let's go see the monkeys!' Hannah shouts. 'They are my favourite!'

They wander round and eventually come to the sign for the monkeys. The monkeys are on an island of their own, so the girls will have to go on a boat. They get in the queue, which is extremely long.

Hannah is ever so excited. 'I just love the monkeys,' she says. 'They are so much like us and so funny to watch.'

They all laugh. Eventually, they reach the start of the queue and it's their turn to embark on the boat. Abigail and Hannah get on first and take a seat. The man helping everyone on shouts, 'Hold on! The boat is full. Please wait for the next boat.'

Jodie and Becky look at one another. Becky says, 'Oh no, we are going to get separated!'

'It's okay,' Jodie says. 'We will be right behind them in another boat.'

They wait on the next boat while watching Abigail and Hannah's boat sail away. By the time Jodie, Becky, and everyone else get on the next boat, they can no longer see Abigail and Hannah. 'I hope we don't lose them,' Becky says.

Abigail and Hannah keep looking back for the other two, but they are nowhere to be seen. Abigail points. 'Look over there, Hannah. There is a monkey with four babies. They are so cute.'

As they sail by, they see monkeys swinging from trees. Some even look as if they are waving at them.

The man steering the boat announces through the microphone, 'Once we get to the other side, we can all get off and walk round the edge of the monkey area. There's an extremely high fence that you can see through. It has a roof, so the monkeys cannot escape and get into trouble.'

They reach the other side. Both Abigail and Hannah climb out and start to follow the others.

Abigail says, 'Let's sit here and watch the monkeys while we wait on Jodie and Becky. Look at that one! He's got a cap on backwards and is making facial expressions as if he's laughing.'

Eventually Jodie and Becky catch up and they all sit for a bit to watch the monkey's antics.

Abigail takes the note from the cap out of her pocket to have another look at it. 'Look,' she says to the others. 'There's another message on the back of it!' She can't believe she never noticed it. 'It says the more you use the teleporter, the more power you will have. All will be revealed.'

Becky shouts, 'Oh, this is exciting! What does it mean, the more power you will have?'

'We need to put things to the test,' Hannah says. 'Let's see,' she says, standing up on the wooden bench. 'I wish I could fly,' she says rather loudly. People walking past turn and stare in her direction. The other three laugh uncontrollably.

Becky says, 'Listen, we need to be careful what we wish for. Remember what happened to me? I ended up at the Disneyland and couldn't get back home.'

Hannah remains standing on the wooden bench. Her wish to fly was not granted.

Abigail then says, 'I wish I could get closer to the monkeys. The baby ones look so cute.' Next thing she knows, she is on the other side of the fence beside the monkeys.

The other three are speechless.

Abigail shouts, 'Help! What's happened?'

By this time, two baby monkeys come over to where she is sitting and start lifting up sections of her hair, the way monkeys do for each other to look for bugs. She falls back on the ground, banging her head slightly as she falls. One monkey is still searching through her hair, while the other one is making a lot of noise as if it's hysterically laughing.

Hannah shouts through the fence, 'Abigail, are you okay? You need to get out of there! What if the mummy or daddy monkeys come over? They might not be so friendly!' Hannah says with panic in her voice, 'We need to get her out of there!'

Abigail makes another wish. 'Please, can you put me back on the other side of the fence beside my friends?' Nothing happens. They wait and wait, but she is still inside with the monkeys. The funny thing is, people are walking by and don't seem to notice that a young girl is in with the monkeys. Just then, a larger monkey moves towards Abigail. She guesses it could be the mummy. The monkey bends over Abigail to have a closer look, making strange noises. Then all the other monkeys come over to see what all the noise is about.

Hannah is shouting at Abigail to get up. Becky and Jodie both shout, 'Run, Abigail!'

Abigail just lies there in shock, too scared to move, afraid that any sudden movement could make matters worse. Suddenly, the mummy monkey picks Abigail up and takes her to an enclosure out of sight.

Chapter 6

Hannah

Hannah stares at the enclosure in disbelief. 'What are we going to do?' she says, almost in tears. 'We can't leave Abigail in that enclosure with the monkeys! We need to get help! We need to find someone who works here to get her out.'

Becky notices the cap and note lying on the other side of the fence. Abigail must have dropped them when she fell. She squeezes her hand through the fence and manages to grab both the note and the cap. She puts them both in her pocket. 'We need these to get home,' she thinks to herself.

They wander round the fence, unable to find anyone who works there. They get as close to the monkey enclosure as possible. They look through the glass enclosure and, to their astonishment, they see Abigail swinging on the ropes with the monkeys. She even has a banana in her hand!

Jodie shouts, 'Look, it's Abigail! What's she doing? She's acting like she is a monkey.'

Just then, a man arrives with a barrow of food for the monkeys. He goes over to unlock the door.

Becky shouts, 'Excuse me! Can you help us? Our friend Abigail is in there! Can you please get her out?'

The man gives them a bemused look as he opens the door and looks in. 'There is no girl in there,' he says, 'only the monkeys.'

They can all quite clearly see Abigail swinging on the ropes. They all shout at her to jump down and come out, but Abigail doesn't appear to hear them and carries on swinging. After a while, she jumps down.

Hannah shouts, 'She's down! She's coming over, I think!'

But Abigail sits down next to a baby monkey and starts searching through its fur, looking for bugs.

'She's acting like a monkey,' Hannah says. 'What's going on?'

The man then comes back out after leaving food for the monkeys and says, 'Right, kids, be on your way. There's no girl in there. Stop wasting my time.' He leaves.

Hannah is screaming at the top of her voice, 'Abigail, can you hear me? You need to get out of there!'

Abigail doesn't even look her way. She's too busy with the baby monkey.

Becky takes the note out of her pocket, opens it and says, 'Oh, I wish I could comfort Abigail. She must be so scared.' The next minute, Becky is also in the enclosure beside Abigail and is swinging on the ropes.

'I don't believe this,' Hannah says. 'Now the two of them are in there! We really need to watch what we say, or we could end up in even more trouble.'

They stand staring through the glass. To their horror, the biggest monkey they have ever seen walks over to Becky, grabs her off the rope and throws her to the floor. Becky lies motionless. The huge monkey then sits on her back as if using Becky as a seat. During this commotion, Abigail doesn't even seem bothered and carries on looking for bugs in the baby monkey's fur.

Hannah is in tears now. 'This is a disaster, Jodie. What are we going to do?'

Jodie says, 'Let's walk round the glass enclosure and see if there's any way we can get them out.'

They walk round several times but can see no openings. Other people that are watching the monkeys don't seem to be able to see Abigail or Becky. It's as if they are invisible.

Becky seems to stir on the floor.

'Oh look,' Hannah says. 'Becky is okay. She is getting up.'

Again, they both shout, 'Becky! Becky, are you okay? Don't worry, we will get you out!'

Becky doesn't react to their shouts. She jumps up and grabs a monkey's legs, holding on to them as the monkey swings from a rope so that she is swinging as well. Then they notice Abigail is eating the food the zookeeper put in for the monkeys.

'Oh my goodness!' Jodie says. 'What is Abigail doing? Surely she's not enjoying eating those scraps of food.'

Hannah turns to Jodie. 'Jodie, have you noticed that although we are screaming at the two of them in there, no one else seems to be asking us what's wrong?

How can that be? They must hear us. The zookeeper heard us when we said Abigail was in there. This just doesn't make sense.'

Hannah and Jodie both sit down on a nearby bench and have a cry. They are both so worried. They start to think that they really shouldn't be messing with all this teleportation stuff, as they really don't know enough about how it all works.

'What if the monkeys hurt them or, worse still, kill them?' Jodie says.

Hannah lets out a half-hearted laugh.

'Well, look at them. They appear to be having fun swinging on those ropes and eating that food. Look at us. We are miserable. We are helpless and so worried.'

They sit and stare at the glassed area of the monkey enclosure where Abigail and Becky are. One of the larger monkeys is swinging on the rope and banging into the window that faces them, as if he's in a bad mood and is trying to scare them away.

'He's going to break that window,' Hannah says, 'if he hits it any harder.'

Jodie jumps up, wondering where the note from the cap is. She remembers Becky had it last. 'I hope the note isn't in that monkey enclosure with them.' They start looking for it, but it's nowhere to be seen.

There's an announcement coming through a loudspeaker. They both stand still to listen. The man is saying that the zoo will be closing in an hour, and asks everyone at the monkey area to make their way to the boating area to be taken back across the water.

Hannah says, 'We really need to get them out. We need to get back into the boat and back to where we started at the dolphin area so we can get back home.' Hannah notices a piece of paper stuck to the fence. It has a sticky lollipop stuck to it. 'Could that be the note?' she wonders. She jumps up and grabs it. She pulls the yucky lollipop off and puts it in the bin next to the bench where Jodie is sitting. 'Jodie!' she shouts. 'It's the note!' Hannah's eyes dart over it. She says, 'I wish all four of us could be back at the dolphin show and ready to be teleported home.'

The next minute, they are all back sitting at the dolphin show again. They look at one another, stunned. Did that wish really just come true?

Abigail says, 'Right, we really better get home.'

They hold hands and start to recite the saying, but there's no rumbling to be heard. They haven't moved. It hasn't worked this time.

'What went wrong?' Hannah says, her voice trembling.

They hear an announcement asking everyone to leave the dolphin area because the park is closing.

'We can't leave,' Jodie says. 'We need to be in the exact same spot where we arrived in order to get back home.'

People start to push by them, giving them dirty looks as if to ask why they are holding everyone up by not following the orderly queue.

'Wait,' Becky says. She almost falls over as a man tries to squeeze by her, trying to make his way to the exit and probably wondering why they are still hanging around. As she stumbles, she notices the note at their feet on the floor. She grabs it and says, 'I think we need to be in possession of this while we recite the saying.' They quickly sit back down and hold hands. Abigail is at one end, and in her free hand she holds the note. They start to recite the words, praying it works...'Please transport me back to the hideaway cave.'

Chapter 7

Becky

They arrive back in the cave with a bump. They look at one another.

'Are we back in the cave?' Becky asks.

'I don't know,' Jodie says. 'Let's check.' She opens the door slowly. 'Yes!' she shouts. 'We are back!'

'Thank goodness,' says Abigail. 'We have one hour before we need to get home. Let's talk about what actually happened today.'

Hannah tells Abigail and Becky how they ended up in the monkey enclosure and were actually acting as if they were monkeys.

Abigail and Becky both laugh. 'We knew what we were doing,' Abigail says. 'We thought it best to act like one of them so they would maybe accept us better and not harm us.'

Jodie turns to Abigail and says, 'Abigail, you were eating the monkey food.'

'No, I wasn't. I was only pretending.'

'But why didn't you come out when the zookeeper unlocked the door?' Becky asks. 'Then I wouldn't have ended up in there with you.'

'I couldn't,' Abigail explains. 'There was a huge monkey watching my every move. I had to be careful so he wouldn't attack me.'

Becky laughs. 'What a day this has been. We better get home. I wonder what tomorrow will bring.'

They get out of the cave and board it up as best they can in the hope that no one else will find it. They run along the water's edge and then climb over the wall that takes them onto the promenade. After arranging to meet at the same time and place tomorrow, they all go their separate ways.

Becky wakes really early the next morning and is up and dressed before anyone else. She can't wait to meet the others. She arrives at the promenade first and sits looking out to sea in deep thought while she waits for the others. One by one, they all arrive.

'Let's go to the cave!' Becky shouts.

They all run along the beach, excited and eager to get there. Today will be another adventure.

They get in the cave and switch all the lanterns and torches on.

Becky says, 'Right, what do we know about this teleporter?'

'We know we must always have two of us for the return journey, as we are not tall enough to press the green button and turn the red lever at the same time,' Jodie says.

'We must hold hands before reciting the saying so we don't get separated,' Abigail adds, 'as it's only the person holding the note that can be transported.'

'Also, the person holding the note must hold on tight to it, because I managed to drop it before I got thrown into the monkey compound,' Becky reminds them.

'Luckily, I found it stuck to the fence,' Hannah says.

'We know if you are holding the note, you can make a wish and it will come true,' Abigail says. 'We know if you are holding the note and make a wish, you are invisible and you can't be heard. And as long as we are linked together by holding hands or linking arms when the wish is made, it affects us all.'

'I also think that even if you have held the note and dropped it by mistake, you remain invisible to other humans,' Becky says. 'Because remember, Abigail, you dropped it when you fell over when that mummy monkey came over to you. We were able to retrieve the note, as it was close to the fence and everyone else who was walking by could not see what was happening to you.'

'We could have a lot of fun with this invisible thing as well as the adventures to different destinations,' Jodie says.

'We probably still have a lot to learn,' Hannah points out.

Becky stands up. 'Can I pick a journey to go on today?'

'Yes,' the rest all say together.

'I would like to go to the biggest toy factory where all the toys come alive,' Becky says.

Jodie squeals, 'Oh, that would be good! Let's get in the teleporter and not waste any time.'

They all jump in and recite the saying. Jodie presses the green button. The teleporter grumbles and shakes, and they are off.

Next thing they know, they are standing in the middle of a huge factory. There are teddy bears, giant dolls, train sets and trucks everywhere. They don't know what to do first. Suddenly, the lights go out and some really dim ones come on. They can hear shutters going down as if the place is shutting.

'What's going on?' Becky asks, rather alarmed. They start to wander round. 'Let's stick together,' Becky insists. 'Let's not have any disasters today.'

They come across a really big doll. Hannah pulls on its long hair, which is pleated, and says, 'Hi, girl, what's your name?'

'Ouch,' says the doll. 'Don't pull my hair.'

The girls all get the fright of their life and cling onto each other.

'Did that doll really speak?' Jodie asks.

'Yes, I did,' says the doll. 'My name is Maxine. Why are you here? As of now, the factory is closed for two weeks for summer holidays. When you girls entered, you caused all the lights to come on. Then, because you all stood still, they went out again and the low-energy ones came back on. You don't need to be afraid, none of the toys will hurt you. We welcome you to come play and enjoy all the toys here. We toys always have so much fun when the big bright lights go out and the shutters go down.'

Hannah tells Maxine the doll that she is sorry for pulling her hair. 'Let's each pick a toy,' she says. 'I would like Maxine.' She lifts her off the shelf.

All of a sudden, there's a huge racket as all the dolls, and even the action men, shout, 'Pick me! Pick me!'

Abigail takes control and shouts, 'You toys are all making too much noise! Please be quiet and the rest of us will pick one of you.' Abigail says that she would like a cuddly dog and wanders over to where all the dogs are. Some are barking. She picks a black and white one. As she goes over to the dog, it wags its tail.

'Woof, woof. Thank you for choosing me! My name is Charlie. I can run fast and fetch anything you want.'

Becky decides she wants one of the dolls that looks like a fairy. 'Thank you for choosing me, dear,' the fairy says. 'I'm a fairy godmother. My name is Sparkle.' Becky smiles at the fairy, chuffed with her choice.

Jodie decides to choose a very large teddy bear. The bear says in a very loud voice, 'Hi, my name is Bruno. I'm ever so strong. I will look after you.' Jodie smiles after she gets over the fright from his very loud voice.

'Okay,' Becky says, 'Let's all go to the area with the swings. We can take our toys and all play together.'

Off they run with Maxine the doll, Sparkle the fairy, Charlie the dog and Bruno the teddy bear.

Hannah puts Maxine onto one of the swings. It has a bar across it to keep her safe. Maxine shouts, 'Higher! Higher, Hannah!' as Hannah pushes and pushes her.

Abigail is on the artificial grass with Charlie the dog. She is training him to sit and to give her a paw.

Jodie is with Bruno the teddy bear. They both climb onto the chute. Bruno slides down first, followed by Jodie, who crashes into him at the bottom. Bruno roars loudly, 'Be careful!' Jodie apologises. She is still a bit afraid of him.

Becky is walking hand-in-hand with Sparkle the fairy. Sparkle asks Becky if there is anything she would like to wish for. 'I can make dreams come true,' Sparkle says.

Becky says, 'I wish I could look as pretty as you.'

Sparkle says, 'You are very pretty.'

'I would like to have blonde hair just like you,' Becky says, 'and be wearing

108

the same pretty dress and have wings just like you.'

Sparkle tells Becky to shut her eyes and wait a moment. She waves her wand and casts a spell to make Becky look like her. 'Open your eyes,' Sparkle says.

Becky looks down. She is wearing a dress that looks just like Sparkle's. She has blonde hair instead of her normal black, and now has her own set of wings and a wand. She squeals with laughter. 'Oh, I look just like Sparkle!' she shouts to the others.

'Oh, my,' Abigail says from the back. 'You look like twins. You are the same height and you both have blonde hair and a set of wings.'

Sparkle turns to Becky. 'Come with me,' she says, 'and we will have some fun.'

They all have a great time playing with the toys.

Jodie looks at her watch. 'Listen, girls, we better think about getting back to the cave.'

Abigail shouts, 'Oh no! We don't have the note with the instructions to get home!'

Maxine the doll, who has a little bag attached to her, shouts, 'Is this what you are looking for?' and holds it in the air. 'Well, you need to get it off me!'

Maxine starts to run about the factory. Jodie almost catches her, but then Maxine throws the note to Charlie the dog, who can dart and run very fast. Next, Bruno joins in. He just stands still with it. Everyone is too afraid to go near him, as he's a bit grumpy.

Abigail shouts, 'Please, toys, give us the note! We really need to get back home. We will be late and get into trouble.'

Becky says, 'Wait a minute. Sparkle, can you help us?'

'Unfortunately, I can't,' Sparkle says. 'There's only one wish granted each day, and you already used it. That's it till tomorrow.'

Bruno then comes over. 'I'm really sorry,' he says. 'Here is your note. We will let you go home. We have enjoyed your company.'

'Right,' Becky says. 'Sparkle, can you quickly wave your wand and put me back in my normal clothes as well as getting rid of my blonde hair and wings?'

'I'm sorry,' Sparkle says. 'Only one wish per day, though you will be able to do it yourself tomorrow. Just wave the wand and make your wish. You will need to wait till 11:30 a.m., as that's when I granted your wish today.'

'Okay,' Becky says. 'But what will my mum say?'

Abigail, looking at her watch, says, 'Listen, girls, we will worry about Becky's problem when we get back. Let's link up. Where's the note? Let's read what it says.' Abigail reads it.

It's the usual phrase, but there is a separate message at the bottom of the page. It says: Now that you have used the teleporter to go to three different destinations, you are able to make time stand still. Just press the yellow button before setting off on your journey. As time goes on, you will discover extra powers and things you are able to do. I hope you enjoyed being invisible at times whilst at the zoo—it saved you from a lot of trouble.

Chapter 8

Jodie

They arrive back in the cave safely, with Becky still looking like Sparkle.

'How can I go home like this?' Becky says. 'I'm dressed like a fairy and have blonde hair and a set of wings.'

Jodie suggests, 'Why don't you come and stay at my house tonight? My mum and dad are away for a few days and my gran is looking after me. My gran won't notice your hair.'

'Great, I will phone my mum and ask if it's okay,' Becky says. Her mum agrees, so at least her problem is solved for now. Hopefully when she makes her wish tomorrow, she will be back to her normal self.

Abigail and Hannah go their separate ways while Jodie and Becky head off together to Jodie's house. Becky gets a few cheeky comments from a group of boys they pass on the way. 'Hey!' they shout. 'Why are you dressed like a fairy? It's not Halloween yet.'

Becky and Jodie both giggle and run on. They wouldn't know where to begin to try and explain.

Jodie says, 'We will tell my gran you were at a fancy-dress party today and didn't have time to go home and get changed. Then tomorrow you can make your wish to be back to your normal self.'

The plan works. The next morning, they have breakfast early before Jodie's gran is even up. They then go back to Jodie's room, where they plan to stay until 11:30. When the time comes, Becky makes her wish and, as if by magic, she is back to her normal self.

They then head down to the cave. Abigail and Hannah are already there.

Jodie asks, 'Can I choose the destination today?'

'Yes!' they all shout at once.

Abigail says, 'Remember, we now have the power to make time stand still by pressing the yellow button. This means if we leave at noon today, we can stay as long as we want and when we return it will still be noon.'

Jodie says, 'I would like to go to an enchanted forest where elves and fairies live and magical things happen.'

'That sounds brilliant!' Abigail screams. 'Hurry up, let's get in!'

When they are all in the teleporter, Abigail presses the yellow button, and it lights up with a message saying that time will stand still. They all cheer at once. 'This is going to be so much fun! We can stay as long as we want, and we won't be missed!'

Hannah presses the green button while Jodie says, 'Please transport us to an enchanted forest where fairies and elves live and magical things happen.' Next thing they know, they are at the edge of a forest surrounded by tress and high hedges.

'Look,' Jodie says, pointing. 'There's a small red wooden gate over there. Do you think that's the entrance?' They all run over. Jodie opens the gate slowly and it makes a loud creaking noise. 'Follow me, everyone,' she says as she leads the way.

They follow the pathway. There's not much to see except lots and lots of tress. The path seems to bend round a corner.

When they get around, they are amazed to see that the whole place is lit up in all the colours of the rainbow. There are fairies singing while flying around, elves on the ground playing with a ball, and toadstools that appear to have faces. As they go past, one of the toadstools shouts, 'Hi! My name is Thomas!'

They all scream and grab onto one another due to the fright they got.

'It's okay, I won't hurt you,' Thomas says. 'We are all friendly here. Come over, don't be afraid.'

They all slowly walk over, still a bit unsure of the talking toadstool.

'What are your names? Why are you here?'

Abigail finds her voice. 'I'm Abigail and this is Jodie, Hannah and Becky.' She doesn't tell him about the teleporter because she wants it to remain their secret. 'We were just out for a walk and noticed the red gate. We wondered what there was to see.'

'You can't be disappointed, then,' Thomas laughs. 'This is the most magical place in the whole world. Everyone is happy here. There is so much to see and do. Let me show you around. Follow me.' He points to the trees. 'Now if you look closely at all the trees, you will see they all have faces on them. This is to let you know who lives there. Look, that one is a soldier. Then there's a ballerina over there, and a cat, cobbler, mouse, fisherman, schoolteacher…the list goes on. There are over a hundred people living here.'

He points in another direction and says, 'Look, come this way. There's a beautiful lake which is lit up by many lights. The little boats in the water are used by the elves. They don't mind if people who visit want to try them out too. If you take a boat across the water, you will end up on the land of elves. They all live in the same area.'

As they stare out at the water, there are lots of colourful butterflies flying round. Thomas says, 'See that house there in the shape of a shoe? Well, George the cobbler stays there. He's a very quiet, private man. He doesn't like people standing outside his house.' Then he points to the tree house in the corner. 'That's where Miss Clarke stays. She is the schoolteacher. Everyone here goes to school, even the babies and adults. Miss Clarke is very strict and doesn't put up with any nonsense.'

Thomas looks at his watch. 'Oh, I must get back. I have a meeting with the fairies. I have shown you round some of the forest. You can wander round on your own now. Just be pleasant to everyone you meet, and you will be fine.'

They thank Thomas and start to wander round. Suddenly, they hear someone shouting, 'Girls, what are you doing? Who are you? I don't know your names. I'm Miss Clarke. I expect to see you all at my door in an orderly queue in half an hour, as school will be commencing. If you are not here on time, there will be trouble.' She shuts the window of the tree with a bang.

'Oh, I don't know if I like it here anymore,' Becky cries. 'She doesn't sound very nice.'

Hannah reminds them of what Thomas said as long as they are nice to everyone, they will be okay. They plan to come back in half an hour for school. They turn and walk past the shoe house. They see George the cobbler peeking out from behind his curtains, so they wave at him. He then appears at the door.

'Hi, girls. I'm George. Why are you standing outside my house?'

'We were just walking past,' Hannah says. 'This is our first time here.'

'Right, wait there!' George shouts. He comes out to meet them. He is a short man with thick, curly black hair. 'Right, all of you come into my house. I need to fix your shoes.'

'He looks annoyed with us,' Jodie whispers. 'I think we better do as he says.'

They go in. He doesn't have much furniture. In fact, all he has is a sofa and one small lamp that sits on top of a box on the floor in the living room. The rest of the room is covered in shoes. He has what looks like a work bench, which must be where he works on all the shoes.

'I'm very busy just now and there's only twenty minutes before school starts. I need to fix all your shoes very quickly, as you can't be late for Miss Clarke's class,' George says.

They each take their shoes off and all squeeze onto his tiny sofa while he works on their shoes.

He hammers and bangs on their shoes, then polishes them so they can almost see their faces in them. 'Right,' he says, 'You must all come to me once a week so I can fix and polish your shoes. No one here goes around with tatty shoes.'

They each take their shoes back, but for some reason there is only one of Jodie's shoes. 'Where is my other shoe?' Jodie asks.

George looks annoyed. 'What do you mean? They were all sitting together.'

Jodie's other shoe is nowhere to be seen. They all start to look for it.

'Hurry up,' George says. 'We have five minutes before class starts. We will get in trouble if we are late.'

They all start lifting shoes up to see if it's Jodie's. There are so many shoes that it's like trying to find a needle in a haystack. No luck, they can't find it.

George, losing his temper slightly, shouts, 'Just take this one! It looks like your size. Let's hope Miss Clarke doesn't notice.'

Jodie grabs it. It's not even the same colour—it's black and her other shoe is brown, but it fits so it will do.

They all climb down the stairs from the shoe house to get outside.

'Hurry up,' George says as he runs ahead. 'We need to get to class on time.'

They arrive at Miss Clarke's tree house. Already there is a long queue outside. They join the queue behind George.

'Do all these people fit into the tree house at the same time?' Hannah asks.

George replies, 'Well, off course. Miss Clarke's house is huge inside.'

They all follow single file into the tree house. It is massive with lots of desks and chairs. As Jodie walks past Miss Clarke, the teacher shouts, 'Excuse me, young lady, what on earth have you on your feet? Your shoes do not match.'

'I'm sorry,' Jodie replies in a very quiet voice. 'I have lost one of my shoes and George kindly gave me this one.'

'Hey!' shouts a girl from the back of the class. 'That black shoe belongs to me. George was repairing my black shoes for me. Give it back!' The girl goes over to where Jodie is standing and pulls the shoe off her foot with so much force that both Jodie and the girl fall over.

Miss Clarke is not pleased. 'Get up at once, girls,' she says. 'I will not have you disrupting the class. Both of you stand outside my door. I will deal with you both in a minute.' She gives the rest of the class work to do. She then opens the door to where Jodie and the young girl are standing. The young girl's name is Angelina. She is a ballerina.

'Your punishment for disrupting the class will be…let me think,' Miss Clarke says. 'You will go downstairs and wash and dry all the dishes from yesterday. Go now.'

Jodie follows Angelina to the dining room. Angelina marches on ahead, not talking to Jodie.

'Right,' Angelina says. 'Get washing all the dishes. Then dry them and put them away while I go next door and watch some TV.'

'What?' Jodie says. 'You can't leave me to do all the dishes on my own!' She looks at the enormous pile.

'Watch me,' Angelina says. 'It's your fault I'm down here.' She then disappears and leaves Jodie to it.

Class finishes. Abigail, Hannah and Becky are standing outside the tree house, wondering where Jodie is. Abigail says, 'We will have to wait on Jodie.'

Miss Clarke comes to the door. 'Move along, girls. Please don't stand outside my house,' she says, looking most annoyed with them.

They are walking down the hill when they notice a tunnel. There are three steps up to it.

'Let's go and have a look!' Hannah shouts as she runs up the stairs. 'Come on, everyone, let's see where this leads to!'

As they go further, lots of coloured fairy lights start to appear. The walls of the tunnel are painted white, so although they are in a tunnel it is quite bright inside. The fairies are all dancing and singing.

'Hi!' one shouts. 'My name is Shelly. Would you like to join us?'

'Yes, please,' Hannah answers. She is mesmerised by all the little fairies.

They all sing and dance, thoroughly enjoying themselves.

'Would you like to go meet our elf friends who stay across the lake?' one of the fairies asks.

'Yes,' they all reply at once.

'Each of you pair up with one of the fairies. Take their hand and we will fly you across the lake.' Up in the air they go, looking down on the lake that's lit up in every colour of the rainbow. It really is something quite magnificent.

Meanwhile, back at Miss Clarke's house, Jodie has washed, dried and put away all the dishes. Angelina makes an appearance. 'Oh, that was a great film I watched.'

Just then, Miss Clarke appears. 'Right, girls, let that be a lesson to you both. Do not disrupt my class again. You are now free to go home.'

They walk outside. Jodie is really worried. 'Home?' she thinks. 'I don't have a home here.'

To her surprise, Angelina turns and says, 'Nice meeting you, Jodie. See you tomorrow at school.'

Jodie walks down the hill, hoping to meet someone friendly that can help her. Her fingers are all wrinkly from being in the hot, soapy water for so long. She is now tired and hungry. She wasn't able to join the others in the garden at break time for lunch because she was too busy doing dishes.

She starts looking more closely at all the faces on the trees, trying to work out who lives there. Some are obvious and some not so. She stops at one that has a face of a soldier. It was one of the ones Thomas pointed out to them when they first arrived. 'Surely a soldier will help me,' Jodie thinks. She knocks on the door three or four times, but there is no answer. 'He can't be home,' she thinks. Exhausted from her day, she sits down on a log and shuts her eyes, wondering where the others are. After a while, she wakes up with a feeling that someone is there. She looks around but cannot see anyone. Then she notices a white cat at her feet.

'Hello,' the cat says. 'My name is Tabby. What's yours?'

'Jodie,' she replies. 'I've just arrived today with my friends.'

'Ah, yes,' says Tabby. 'You were one of the girls that got in trouble in Miss Clarke's class today. Come with me. I know where your friends went. They went over to elf land. Listen, sit on my back and I will take you to the water's edge to catch a boat.'

Jodie looks down at Tabby. 'Am I not too big to sit on your back?'

'No,' Tabby says. 'I am very strong. Take a seat and I will show you.'

Jodie sits ever so carefully.

'Hold on to my collar!' Tabby shouts.

The next minute, Jodie is jolted backwards and they are off. When they get to the water's edge, Tabby the cat jumps onto one of the boats with Jodie on his back.

'What a beautiful lake,' Jodie says.

'Yes, it always looks like this,' Tabby says. 'There's not much light due to the high trees and hedges, so we put lights everywhere. It does give off lovely colours across the water.'

They arrive at the other side. There are two elves sitting on a bench near the water's edge. Tabby runs over to them.

'Jack, Craig,' he says, 'come over and meet my new friend Jodie.'

'We remember you,' they both say at the same time, 'from Miss Clarke's class.'

'Oh my,' Jodie thinks. 'I'm certainly well-known here.'

'Your friends are over at Gabby's. Her tree house is this way. Gabby is a baker and bakes cakes for everyone. Your friends will be getting a good feed while there.'

Gabby's house is very big, although not as big as Miss Clarke's.

Tabby bangs on the door. 'Gabby, are you there?'

'Yes, Tabby,' she replies. 'Up you come. I have some other guests here too.'

Tabby and Jodie climb the many stairs—forty-five in total. Jodie is out of puff by the time they reach the top.

'This is Jodie,' Tabby says. 'She has been looking for her friends.'

Abigail, Hannah and Becky all run over to give her a big hug.

'We have been worried about you! We thought you were never going to get away from Miss Clarke's house,' Becky says.

Gabby says, 'Right, everyone, come into my kitchen. I have some freshly baked rolls and cakes. Everyone helps themselves.'

Tabby loves visiting Gabby, as she always has plenty of leftovers for him. Tabby makes his excuses and leaves once he's been watered and fed.

'Bye Tabby!' Jodie shouts. 'Thank you for coming to my rescue!'

Gabby asks them if they would like to bake some cakes. They all shout, 'Yes!'

'Right, gather round the table. Each of you take a bowl and a spoon and copy as I do.'

They all have fun baking cakes with Gabby, though there's more flour on them than in their bowls.

'Right, we need to put them in the oven for thirty minutes. Come through to the living room, girls. Have a seat while we wait on the cakes.' Gabby then remembers she needs to go and make a few deliveries. 'Will you be okay till I come back, girls? I won't be long. Remember to keep an eye on the cakes.' Gabby leaves.

The girls are sitting down to rest, asking Jodie what her punishment was, when there's a tap at the window.

'What was that?' Hannah screams. 'How can anyone reach the window? We are forty-five stairs up!'

It happens again. They peek through the blinds.

'It's okay,' Abigail says. 'It's the fairies. They can fly and reach the window.' They all run to the window. Abigail asks, 'What do you want, fairies?'

'Come out and play with us!' one shouts. 'Let's dance and sing round the trees!'

'Okay!' the girls shout. They are having a ball of a time.

Hannah stops in her tracks all of a sudden. There is smoke coming from Gabby's house. 'Oh no!' Hannah shouts. 'The cakes! We have forgotten about them!' They all race inside.

The fairies are shouting, 'You are not qualified to put fires out! We will fly over the lake and bring back the firemen.' By this time, the curtains have caught fire and there is an awful burning smell.

The fairies bring back the firemen. The fire is put out safely just as Gabby returns. 'What has happened here? My house! My lovely house is ruined! You stupid, stupid girls! What happened?'

'It was the cakes,' Abigail tries to explain. 'We forgot about them. We are so sorry! We will help clean up your house.'

The fairies say, 'We will fly and get cleaning products and paint to help too.'

Only the kitchen and part of the living room are badly damaged. They clean, wipe and scrub. Gabby is still in a bad mood, so no one is really talking. Gabby goes downstairs without saying where she is going. The girls all look at one another and laugh.

'How did we manage to forget the cakes?' Abigail says as she opens a cupboard door. She takes a step to look in, and suddenly she is sliding down a chute. She lands with a bump at the bottom, covered in flour. 'Help!' she shouts. 'Somebody help!'

They all lean through the door, trying to see what happened to Abigail. All they can see when they look down is a white cloud of flour.

Hannah says, 'I think this is where Gabby must put all her scraps. If we go downstairs, there must be a door you can open to get in.'

On their way down, they meet Gabby coming up. 'Where are you three going, and where is Abigail?'

'Oh, eh,' Becky says. 'We were looking to see if you were coming. Abigail went with one of the fairies. They wanted Abigail to fly with them to help choose paint.'

They follow her back upstairs. Becky whispers to Hannah, 'What are we going to do? How are we going to get Abigail out?'

Abigail is at the bottom of the waste disposal chute, covered in flour, pastry, margarine and chocolate. 'Well, at least it's not smelly rubbish,' she thinks. 'It's just cake ingredients. I will just have to stay here until the girls can rescue me.'

Becky announces that she will go downstairs to see if she can see the fairies coming back with the paint and cleaning products. Gabby just throws her a dirty look. Becky has a plan. Maybe the fairies can help get Abigail out without Gabby having to know.

Abigail just lies in a heap of flour, pastry, margarine and chocolate, waiting to be rescued.

Chapter 9

Abigail

Abigail awakens all stiff and covered in cake ingredients. She finds a fairy sitting beside her. 'Abigail, I'm here to help you get out,' the fairy says. 'I had to wait till you woke up. Right, take my hand and I will use magic to get us back outside.'

It works. The next minute, they are both outside Gabby's tree house. Both of them are covered in a mess.

'Take my hand again, Abigail. I will take you up to Mrs Harper's house. She is the laundry lady. I'm sure she will be able to help us get cleaned up.'

They arrive at Mrs Harper's house, a boat house which sits on the lake. The fairy chaps her door. 'Mrs Harper, are you there?'

'Yes, little fairy, I will be with you in a moment.' She opens the door and gasps. 'What on earth has happened to you both?'

'Oh, it's a long story,' the fairy says. 'Can we get cleaned up here?'

'Yes,' she answers. 'Come in. We will go up to the top deck.' She tells them to stand still and shut their eyes.

'Why?' asks Abigail.

'Just do as she says,' the fairy tells Abigail.

They both shut their eyes and the next thing they know, they are both in the lake. Mrs Harper has pushed them in the lake and is on the top deck roaring with laughter. 'That's the quick way to clean you two up!'

'Help!' Abigail shouts. 'I can't swim!'

'It's okay,' the fairy says. 'Hold on to me. I will get us both back onto the boat.' They get back on safely.

Mrs Harper says, 'That will teach you not to nosey in cupboards that you shouldn't be in. Right, come with me. Sit in the drying area. It's nice and warm. Your clothes will dry quickly there.'

Meanwhile, back at Gabby's, the girls have finished painting. Gabby's house is back to normal.

'Right, on your way, girls,' Gabby says, shooing them downstairs. They go outside and wonder where Abigail is. They thought she would be waiting outside for them.

'Let's go back across the lake,' Hannah says. 'I want to get as far away from Gabby as possible.' They get in one of the small boats and make their way across the lake.

Chapter 10

Mrs Harper

As Hannah, Becky and Jodie make their way across the lake, they hear shouts coming from a very large boat house. As they look over, they see Abigail and one of the fairies waving and shouting for them to roe over to where the boat house is.

Mrs Harper shouts, 'Climb aboard, girls! I hope you are not covered in flour too. Let's all go down to the lower deck.' They all climb down the stairs and take a seat at the tiny table she has.

'Would you like a drink?' she asks.

'Yes,' they all reply.

'Where are you staying, girls?'

'We don't have anywhere to stay,' Abigail replies.

'Well, why don't you all stay with me? I have three bedrooms. One is mine and the other two have bunkbeds. You are welcome to stay as long as you like.'

The girls all cheer. 'Thank you so much,' Hannah replies.

'You will need to help me, though, as I'm very busy at the moment. In return for your help, you can stay and get all your meals for free.'

'What would you like us to do?' asks Jodie

'Well,' Mrs Harper replies, 'I do everyone's washing. It has to be collected, washed, ironed and taken back again. With the five of us in the boat, there should be room for five laundry bags, so we can go to five houses before coming back here. Right, girls, no time like the present. Let's get in one of the small boats and get started.'

They all climb into the boat and Mrs Harper roes them across the lake. 'Okay, everyone out!' Mrs Harper shouts rather loudly. 'We can do one house each. Now remember, only accept one bag as there won't be room for any more.' She points to Abigail. 'Right, along you go to Miss Clarke's.'

'Oh, the schoolteacher,' Abigail replies, remembering how she treated Jodie.

'Yes, hurry along, as we only have three hours before school.'

Off Abigail goes and chaps Miss Clarke's door. She appears at the door in her dressing gown, slippers and hair rollers. Abigail starts to explain that's she come for the washing, but finds herself starting to laugh at the way Miss Clarke looks.

Miss Clarke is not amused. 'What are you laughing at, child?' she says.

'Eh, nothing,' Abigail replies, realising she better stop because Miss Clarke looks angry.

'You better come in then. My laundry is on the floor, follow me.'

Abigail climbs the many stairs.

'Right, take those three bags,' Miss Clarke says.

'I can't,' Abigail says. 'I am only allowed to take one at a time.'

Miss Clarke turns round so quickly that Abigail feels a draught swish past her.

'Did you say "no," young girl? Right, come with me.'

Abigail follows her up two steps to another room. There is a desk and a chair in it.

'Sit there,' Miss Clarke says. She throws a pen and paper on the desk and tells Abigail to write five hundred times 'I must not be cheeky to my schoolteacher. I must respect her at all times.' Abigail shouts, 'But I'm only doing as Mrs Harper told me!'

'Be quiet, stupid girl. Get on with it.' She bangs the door shut as she leaves the room.

Abigail can hear her locking the door. 'Oh no,' Abigail thinks. 'What am I going to do? She's locked me in here till I complete my lines. I better write as fast as I can.'

Jodie has been sent to George the cobbler. She chaps on the door. He peeks out from behind the curtains to see who is at his door. When he sees it's Jodie, he opens the door. Jodie says that she's there for his washing.

'Come in,' he says. 'I keep it in the shed in the garden. Feel free to go and fetch it.'

Jodie thinks, 'George can be real rude. You would think he would have it ready for collection.' She makes her way out to the shed. The door is slightly ajar. She pulls it open wide and steps in. As she does, the most enormous pile of shoes comes tumbling down on top of her. She starts to throw the shoes one by one, trying to get out from under the mound that has come down on top of her. The more she throws, the more that come tumbling down. George has shoes on shelves, hanging from the ceiling and all over the floor. What a mess.

George comes to the back door and shouts, 'Jodie, have you got the washing?'

Jodie tries to shout back, but her voice is muffled as she is buried beneath all the shoes, and more are still falling.

George cannot hear her reply so assumes she must have gotten the washing and left already.

Mrs Harper sends Becky to Belinda the ballerina. Belinda's house is very pretty with lots of colourful lights all round it.

She goes to the door and chaps. There is a pair of beautiful dancing shoes sitting at the door. Becky sits down on the step and tries them on. She stands up and starts to dance, pretending to be a ballerina, just as Belinda opens the door.

'Why have you got my shoes on?' she snaps. 'I have just cleaned and mended them!'

'Oh, I was trying them on,' replies Becky, rather embarrassed at getting caught.

Belinda smiles. 'You are actually a good dancer. I'm doing a show in half an hour, and we are one girl short. Could you help me out?'

'Oh, but I wouldn't know what to do,' Becky replies rather worriedly.

'I will teach you,' Belinda says. 'Come with me.'

'I'm here for your washing, though.'

'Forget the washing! This will be so much more fun.'

Meanwhile, Mrs Harper turns to Hannah. 'Okay, can you go to Gabby's? One of the fairies will take you back across the water.'

'Eeek,' Hannah thinks to herself. 'Of all the people that could need washing collected, today it has to be Gabby.'

One of the fairies takes her by the hand and they quickly fly back across. Hannah knocks on the door. She can hear Gabby coming down the stairs. Hannah's heart starts to beat faster and faster at the thought of being confronted by her again.

Gabby opens the door with a big smile on her face. 'Yes, dear, what can I do for you?'

'I've come for your washing. Mrs Harper has sent me.'

'You better come in, then.' She tells Hannah to wait at the bottom of the stairs while she fetches it. Gabby starts to throw down big bundles of the washing, but they are not in bags. 'Here, catch!' she shouts. 'You can bag them up.'

'What a mess! There is washing everywhere,' Hannah thinks. She starts to put the dirty washing in the bag. The bag gets filled up very quickly. 'My bag is full!' Hannah shouts, but Gabby keeps on throwing more and more at her while she squeals with laughter. Hannah thinks, 'This woman is crazy. I'm out of here.' She grabs what's in the bag and runs. She trips and falls over, bangs her head and knocks herself out cold. She's lying outside Gabby's house. Some of the dirty washing has fallen out of the bag and is lying on top of her. Gabby has now got the window open and is throwing even more washing down, which is landing on top of poor Hannah. She is covered in so much washing that she's hardly visible. Jodie manages to make her way out from underneath all the shoes. She brushes herself down, as she is covered in dust, and then puts her hand in her pocket to see if she has a hanky. While her hand is in her pocket, she says out loud, 'I wish the four of us could be back together. Then we could link up and say the phrase to get out of here.' She doesn't have a hanky but has the note for the return journey. Her wish comes true. The four girls are now outside Gabby's house, all looking a bit worse for wear. Abigail's hand hurts from writing all the lines, Jodie is covered in dust from being at the bottom of a heap of shoes, Becky's toes hurt from helping out Belinda the ballerina and Hannah's head hurts from banging it when she fell over.

Jodie says, 'Let's get out of here.'

'Yes!' they all shout.

They link arms and say the phrase…next thing they know, they are safely back in the cave.

Chapter 11

Robyn

The teleporter bumps down into the cave with the usual rumbles. They all climb out.

'Well, that was some journey,' Abigail says. She checks her watch and sees that it is still noon. Time really did stand still.

Hannah suggests that they all gather round and chat about all that went on in the enchanted forest. They swap stories and have a good old laugh.

Hannah shouts, 'Where will we go tomorrow?'

They all make suggestions but none they can all agree on.

Then Abigail suggests, 'Why don't we try and find out where Robyn, the inventor of the teleporter, went? His note did say "If you are reading this, it's due to something going wrong on my journey as I obviously have not returned." Let's get that old case back out again to look at his books.'

Hannah grabs the case from the table, and they all gather round. Becky takes the book on teleporters, checking for any new information, while Jodie looks at the book on space. There's nothing in either of the books to suggest where Robyn could have chosen to go.

Suddenly, Abigail jumps up all excited.

'Listen! All we have to do is get in the teleporter and tell it to take us where Robyn the inventor chose to go.'

Hannah screams, 'Brilliant, Abigail! Why didn't I think of that?'

They all agree to home to get washed, changed and fed. They agree to meet up tomorrow morning at ten o'clock to go look for Robyn.

Tomorrow arrives and they are all back at the cave.

'Let's get in quickly!' Jodie screams. 'Let's find out where Robyn went!'

Hannah says, 'I will press the green button. Abigail, you say where we want to go and Jodie, you see to making time stand still again just in case we are away for a while.'

Abigail says in a loud, clear voice, 'Please take us to where Robyn the inventor chose to go.'

The teleporter grumbles while it lifts off. They arrive with a bump and wait till the teleporter stops shaking before getting out. Becky opens the door cautiously and steps out first.

'Where are we?' Jodie asks.

'Not sure yet,' Becky replies.

The rest of them follow her out. There is a staircase in front of them. It has a sign saying 'this way.'

'This way to what?' Becky remarks.

'Let's go and see!' Abigail shouts while starting to climb the stairs.

The rest of them follow behind. They get to the top. There is a black door facing them, with a sign on it saying 'welcome to the land of all things magical.' Abigail opens the door slowly. It is stiff and creaks a lot as it opens. They step inside. It's as if they have stepped into another world. There are lots of magicians all practising their magic: a man pretending to saw a woman in half, a woman pulling a never-ending scarf from a small hat, and a man producing rabbits from his pockets.

'Oh, this is wonderful!' Becky cries. 'We can learn some magic whilst we look for Robyn.'

They wander over to the man producing the rabbits and ask if he knows a man called Robyn. 'Why, yes,' the man says. 'I know several. Which one are you looking for?'

'We only know him as Robyn,' they tell him.

The man laughs and taps Becky on the head. Suddenly she is holding a tiny white rabbit. They all go over to stroke it.

'Can you put him down on the ground now? He will run to find his friends. That rabbit's work is done for the day.'

They say goodbye to the rabbit man and continue to walk round. When they come to the man who is sawing the woman in half, they stand and watch. He splits up the boxes that she was in. Her head is in one, her body in another and her legs in the third box.

'How can this be possible?' Hannah says.

'Would one of you like to try?' he asks. Becky puts her hand straight up in the air. 'Please, let me try.'

Becky gets in the box. The man saws through until Becky is in three pieces. They all laugh and cheer.

He then says, 'Now let me make her disappear!' He throws a curtain over the three boxes, says his magic words, takes the curtain off and Becky is gone. Where to, none of them can work out.

Jodie, panicking, shouts, 'Can you bring her back now, please?'

'Not yet,' he replies. 'It will spoil the magic trick. Go away and enjoy yourselves. Come back in a little while and your friend will be here waiting for you.'

Meanwhile, Becky seems to have fallen through some type of trap door and landed on top of an enormous bean bag. There appears to be a lot of trap door openings, with people falling through onto more bean bags. It is quite funny to watch.

A young girl falls onto a bean bag next to her. 'Hi,' she says. 'What's your name?'

'I'm Becky,' she replies. 'I'm here with my three friends. We are looking for a man called Robyn.'

'My name is Laura,' the young girl tells Becky. 'Follow me. We need to wait till the coast is clear before we show our faces again.'

Jodie, Hannah and Abigail walk past a woman sitting on the ground with a large crystal ball. 'Come over, girls,' she beckons. They walk towards the woman. She tells them to sit beside her and to place their right hand on top of the crystal ball and shut their eyes. 'Right,' she says, 'each of you make a wish and they will come true.' Although no one speaks, they are all thinking that it's a load of rubbish. She tells them to keep their eyes closed and to say their wish only inside their heads.

Abigail wishes she could fly. Next thing she knows, she is up in the sky flying around. She keeps falling back down, though, as she hasn't quite gotten the hang of it. Every time she tries to stand and walk normally, up and away she goes again.

Jodie thinks, 'I'm going to wish for something silly.' She wishes she was a gymnast and suddenly she is upside down and walking round on her hands. Every time she tries to stand up properly, she falls over headfirst and lands on her hands upside down.

Hannah has trouble thinking what to wish for and decides to make it simple. She wishes she could be taller, as she is fed up with being so much smaller than her friends. Hannah stands up and realises she can see for miles. She has become a giant and is towering above even the tallest of adults. 'Oh, my goodness,' she says. 'I didn't mean to be this tall.' She looks down. Even her hands and feet are enormous. She begins to panic. 'Where's that woman with the crystal ball? She needs to put me back to my normal size! This is ridiculous!' The woman is nowhere to be seen.

Meanwhile, back under the trap door, Becky asks Laura, 'Do you work here?'

'I live here,' replies Laura, 'with my family. My dad is the man who saws people in half. Well, in three pieces, actually. We have been here for many years.'

All of a sudden, there is a loud bang. 'Quick!' Laura says to Becky. 'The door that leads to the secret passageway is now open for us to make our way back out. Follow me.'

They eventually reach a queue of about ten people who are all waiting to go through the door. The person at the front is a small boy who doesn't seem to be able to open the door. The door is stuck.

The boy shouts, 'It won't budge!'

Laura steps forward. 'Hold on, I will shout up to my dad for help.'

Becky asks, 'Do you not have a mobile? You could phone him.'

'Mobiles don't work in the land of all things magical,' she replies. 'We will just have to wait to be rescued.'

Becky is not happy. She was so happy when she arrived at the land of all things magical, but now she is stuck underground with a load of people she doesn't know and a lot of beanbags. She had wanted to go exploring.

Abigail still doesn't have the hang of flying. She has bumped her head several times now and given herself sore knees by landing with a thud on the ground. Finally, she manages for the first time to land on her feet. She stands still, trying to work out what she is doing wrong. 'Right,' she says, 'Can you fly me back over to the man that was sawing Becky into three pieces? Nice and slowly. Oh, and not too high in the sky, please.' Her feet lift off the ground and she ever so gently floats up in the air, then goes forward whilst picking up a little speed. 'This is better,' she thinks to herself. 'No more sudden movements. I must need to explain better as to what I want.' She lands on her two feet again, right beside the magician who does the sawing. She asks him if he has seen Becky. Abigail's feet start to lift off the ground. She is hovering. 'No, I don't want to fly at the moment. Put me back down, please. I want to stay here and wait on Becky.' She has lifted off the ground again a little, but not high in the sky.

The magician says, 'No, sorry. No one has come back from the secret passageway yet. There seems to be a problem with the door. We are waiting on help to come.'

Jodie is still walking around on her hands, doing handstands and cartwheels constantly. At first she thought it was funny, but now her hands are sore. There are lots of tiny stones stuck to the palms of her hands. She manages to remain still for a second. 'Okay,' she shouts, 'I want to be a gymnast but not every second. Can I please have some time when I can walk around normally?' She does three more cartwheels in a row before landing right side up. 'At last,' she thinks. 'I'm up the right way round, although for how long I don't know.' She decides to go back and try to find the magician who saws people. She gets there and sees Abigail hovering with her feet off the ground.

Jodie laughs. 'What's happened to you?' Just as she gets the words out of her mouth, Jodie starts doing more cartwheels and handstands.

Abigail shouts, 'Don't fool around, Jodie! Help me get firmly back on the ground!'

By now Jodie is back standing on her feet again. 'I would if I could, Abigail, but my wish was to be a gymnast and

I'm constantly doing cartwheels and handstands. It will stop for a short time but then it starts again.'

'Oh,' Abigail says. 'I wished I could fly and, like your gymnastics, it comes and goes. Right now I can't seem to get my feet to stay on the ground.' They both fall into fits of laughter. 'Why did we wish for silly things?' Abigail laughs.

Suddenly they hear a thud, thud noise coming towards them.

'What on earth is that noise?' Abigail shouts in a panic-stricken voice.

They both turn round, and to their amazement, Hannah is walking towards them. She is enormous, with massive feet and hands. She is almost as tall as some of the buildings.

Jodie shouts, 'Hannah, what has happened to you?'

'I wished I was taller, but I had no idea I was going to end up being a giant!' She presses down on Abigail's head and Abigail's feet touch the ground. She flips Jodie back round the right way using only one finger. 'Where is Becky?' she asks.

'She is stuck underground,' Abigail says. 'She fell through a trap door when the magician made her disappear and now the door is stuck.'

'Where is this door to the secret passageway?' Hannah asks the magician. 'I'm sure with the strength I have at the moment, I will be able to open it.'

The magician leads the way. With one tug, Hannah manages to open the door and everyone who was stuck underground starts to climb out, including Becky.

'Right,' Hannah says. 'We need to stick together. No more separate wishes. There are now two people we are looking for—Robyn and the woman with the large crystal ball, so she can put us back to normal.'

They decide to link arms so they will stay together, though they can't link

Hannah's as she is too tall. They grab hold of the bottom of her leg instead.

Abigail's feet lift off the ground. She takes the rest of them with her, including Hannah the giant. They have to fly high in the sky so Hannah doesn't get dragged along the ground. They all shriek with laughter.

Becky shouts, 'Abigail, do something! Get us back on the ground! We are up too high!'

Abigail shouts, 'Please take us all back down to the ground, gently and safely!' Hannah arrives back to the ground first due to her body being so long. The rest fall on top of her. 'This is so funny,' Abigail says. 'I must admit, when I was flying on my own I was a bit scared, but when we are all together it's so much more fun.'

Jodie says, 'Quick, link arms just in case Abigail takes off again.'

Just before they link arms, Jodie starts doing cartwheels and handstands again and is now standing on her hands. The rest are all laughing. Hannah, being the giant she is, tips Jodie back up the right way again. They link back up.

'Let's go looking for Robyn again,' Abigail pipes up. 'That's why we came, after all.'

They ask several different people but seem unable to find the correct Robyn. They decide to have a seat on a bench, though Hannah has to stand because she's so big.

Hannah is looking into the distance and is in a world of her own. 'Look,' she says, pointing. 'There's a man down by the bridge. He looks like he has a teleporter just like the two back at the cave!' The others stretch their necks to try to see, but they are too low. 'Follow me!' Hannah shouts. 'It's got to be him!' They follow Hannah to the bridge and, sure enough, there is a man standing on the bridge next to what looks like a teleporter.

Abigail says, 'Hello, is your name Robyn, by any chance?'

'Why, no,' he replies. 'My name is Ben, but I do know a Robyn. I'm trying to mend this machine of his. He's away getting some tools for me. Take a seat on that log there and wait for him. He won't be long.' They all sit, except for poor Hannah. 'How do you know Robyn?' Ben asks.

Becky quickly replies, 'He's just an old friend.' She doesn't want to say too much to this man, as they don't know him very well.

'Fair enough,' he says as he starts to fiddle about with the teleporter.

Eventually, a man walks towards them. He shouts, 'Ben, I think I've got all the tools you will need!'

'Thanks,' Ben replies. 'Hey, some friends of yours are waiting over there for you!' he shouts back.

Robyn walks over to where the girls are. 'Hi. How can I help you?'

Jodie speaks first. 'Are you the Robyn that invented the teleporters that are on the beach in the cave?'

'Why, yes I am. How do you know about them?' he asks.

Jodie explains, 'We came across them and have been on many journeys. We asked the teleporter to take us to where Robyn the inventor went, and we ended up here in the land of all things magical.'

'Oh, that's the best news I've heard all day! You can take me back home with you. I couldn't get back because I lost the instructions for my return journey. I have been here for five-and-a-half years! I thought I would never get home. I've spent all my time trying to build a new teleporter. My friend Ben has been helping me, but we haven't managed to get it working. Do you have instructions to get back home?'

They all look at one another. 'Who has them?' Becky shouts. 'Not me,' they all say at once. Jodie starts to do handstands again.

Robyn looks at her and laughs. 'Why does your friend keep doing handstands?' Becky explains about the woman with the crystal ball. He says, 'Right, first thing's first, follow me. I know where she lives and she will get you all back to normal.'

They all follow Robyn, with Jodie walking on her hands. A piece of paper falls out of her pocket just as a gust of wind comes from nowhere, and the wind blows the paper up in the air. Hannah, being the giant she is, tries to stretch and catch it but misses. It's gone. They all stare in horror.

'Hold on!' Abigail shouts. 'I can fly after it! Please make me fly after that piece of paper and catch it.' Abigail starts to hover, then up and away she goes. She catches the paper and makes her way back to the others.

Robyn takes them to the woman with the crystal ball and she puts them all back to normal.

'Could she not use magic to send you home, Robyn?'asks Jodie.

'No,' Robyn says. 'The magic only works here in this land. Where's the note?' Abigail hands it to Robyn and he reads it. 'It says "For your return journey, you must go back to where you started." That means we need to go through the black door and down to the bottom of the steps.'

They do just that, say the magic words, and suddenly they are all inside the teleporter. Robyn turns the handle and presses the button at the same time because he's tall. Abigail asks to be taken back to the cave on the beach. They arrive with their usual bump and then climb out.

Robyn thanks them for coming to find him. 'You do know the teleporter is not completely developed, right? There's lots more I want it to be able to do. I need to work on it and make some adjustments to make it even better, so I'm afraid there will be no more journeys for a while. But please come back and visit me to see how things develop. I think you will be pleasantly surprised. I have loads of ideas to make the teleporter even better.'

'Oh, we will!' the girls all scream at once.

'Well, give me at least six months to work on it,' Robyn says. 'Come back when you are on your Christmas holidays and we will have some splendid adventures!'

Printed in Great Britain
by Amazon

22880543R00109